This item is no longer property
of Pima County Public Library
Sale of this item benefited the Library

JAN 2013

W9-BMO-556

Dear Parent:

Congratulations! Your child is taking the first steps on an exciting journey. The destination? Independent reading!

STEP INTO READING® will help your child get there. The program offers five steps to reading success. Each step includes fun stories and colorful art. There are also Step into Reading Sticker Books, Step into Reading Math Readers, Step into Reading Phonics Readers, Step into Reading Write-In Readers, and Step into Reading Phonics Boxed Sets—a complete literacy program with something for every child.

Learning to Read, Step by Step!

Ready to Read **Preschool–Kindergarten**
• big type and easy words • rhyme and rhythm • picture clues
For children who know the alphabet and are eager to begin reading.

Reading with Help **Preschool–Grade 1**
• basic vocabulary • short sentences • simple stories
For children who recognize familiar words and sound out new words with help.

Reading on Your Own **Grades 1–3**
• engaging characters • easy-to-follow plots • popular topics
For children who are ready to read on their own.

Reading Paragraphs **Grades 2–3**
• challenging vocabulary • short paragraphs • exciting stories
For newly independent readers who read simple sentences with confidence.

Ready for Chapters **Grades 2–4**
• chapters • longer paragraphs • full-color art
For children who want to take the plunge into chapter books but still like colorful pictures.

STEP INTO READING® is designed to give every child a successful reading experience. The grade levels are only guides. Children can progress through the steps at their own speed, developing confidence in their reading, no matter what their grade.

Remember, a lifetime love of reading starts with a single step!

© 2013 Viacom International Inc. All rights reserved. Published in the United States by Random House Children's Books, a division of Random House, Inc., 1745 Broadway, New York, NY 10019, and in Canada by Random House of Canada Limited, Toronto. Step into Reading, Random House, and the Random House colophon are registered trademarks of Random House, Inc. Nickelodeon, Team Umizoomi, and all related titles, logos, and characters are trademarks of Viacom International Inc.

Visit us on the Web!
StepIntoReading.com

Educators and librarians, for a variety of teaching tools, visit us at
RHTeachersLibrarians.com

ISBN: 978-0-449-81436-9 (trade) – ISBN: 978-0-375-97157-0 (lib. bdg.)

Printed in the United States of America

10 9 8 7 6 5 4 3 2 1

Random House Children's Books supports the First Amendment and celebrates the right to read.

STEP INTO READING®

nickelodeon TEAM UMIZOOMI™

DOG DAYS

Based on the teleplay "Buster the Lost Dog" by
Clark Stubbs
Illustrated by Lorraine O'Connell

Random House New York

Team Umizoomi plays with Buster the dog.

Geo throws a ball.

Buster chases it.

The ball goes
into a truck.

Buster jumps
into the truck.

Bot sees tools
in the truck.

The truck is going to a work site.

UmiCar can drive
to the work site!

UmiCar jumps
over a mud puddle.

UmiCar stops
at a red light.

A green light means go.

Go, UmiCar, go!

Oh, no!

The bridge is broken!

Geo can fix the bridge with his Super Shapes!

Geo fixed the bridge!

Go, UmiCar, go!

Team Umizoomi is at the work site.

Buster is stuck
in the bucket!

Buster jumps out
of the bucket.

Team Umizoomi
and Buster
ride down a slide.

Team Umizoomi rides
Buster to the park.

Team Umizoomi and Buster are back at the park.

Everybody Crazy Shake!

Hooray!